NELLIE
Learns Patience

Author
Jessica Almeida

Illustrator
Justine Tobin

Tellwell Talent
www.tellwell.ca

ISBN
978-0-2288-3572-1 (Hardcover)
978-0-2288-3571-4 (Paperback)

For Liam and Kennedy

Keep reading – Never stop learning –
Knowledge is everything

Love you both,
Mommy xo

Nellie is a little girl who lives with her mommy and daddy. Her papa lives next door, and Papa has a H-U-G-E vegetable garden.

Every afternoon, Nellie waits by her window to watch for her Papa's blue car to come home from work. Once she spots it, she eagerly runs over and asks, "Papa, can I pick a vegetable from your garden?"

"Not yet," Papa says. "They need more time to grow. We must be patient."

"Okay," Nellie replies and walks sadly back to her house.

The next day, Nellie sees Papa's blue car driving towards his house. She runs next door to see him and again asks, "Papa, can I pick a vegetable from your garden?"

"Not yet," Papa replies. "They need more time to grow. If we pick them too soon, the vegetables will be too small to eat and enjoy. We must be patient."

Little Nellie does not want to wait. The next day, before her Papa gets home from work, she decides to sneak over to his garden. No one is around, so she picks a carrot. To her surprise, the carrot is very tiny.

"One of these vegetables must be ready to be picked," Nellie thinks. So, she goes over to the radishes, picks one and to her disbelief it too is very tiny.

Nellie hears her Papa's car driving down the street, so she quickly runs back to her house tracking dirt behind her.

As Papa gets out of his car, he walks over to his garden and notices footprints in the dirt. Beside the footprints lie the tiny carrot and the tiny radish that Nellie picked. He knows someone has been in the garden. He also notices the trail of dirt from the garden leads right to Nellie's house. He doesn't say anything in hopes she learns a lesson.

Some time goes by where Nellie stays in her house for fear of getting in trouble for what she did.

One afternoon by the window, she sees Papa's blue car coming up the street. Papa gets out of his car, looks over at his garden and then walks right over to Nellie's house.

Nellie hears Papa knock on the door. She nervously opens it.

Papa looks at her with a big smile and says, "Nellie, would you like to come over and pick some vegetables with me? The garden is ready."

Nellie's frown quickly turns upside down as she jumps and screams, "YES!"

They walk over to his garden together and Nellie picks a carrot. It is H-U-G-E!

She looks up at Papa with guilt and says, "Papa, it was me who touched your garden before and I'm truly very sorry."

Papa is a smart man. He knows it was Nellie from the dirt trail she left behind. He looks at her and says, "It's okay, Nellie. Thank you for telling me. Just remember, good things take time, which is why we must learn to be patient."

Papa gives Nellie a big bear hug and they both continue to pick cucumbers, lettuce, onions, peppers and tomatoes. Everything they pick is H-U-G-E!

Nellie struggles to carry the full basket inside Papa's house where they enjoy a big colorful salad made from their freshly picked vegetables.

– THE END –

CPSIA information can be obtained
at www.ICGtesting.com
Printed in the USA
LVHW071629030221
678276LV00015B/548

9 780228 835721